Dear Parent:
Your child's love of reading starts here!

Every child learns to read in a different way and at his or her own speed. You can help your young reader improve and become more confident by encouraging his or her own interests and abilities. You can also guide your child's spiritual development by reading stories with biblical values and Bible stories, like I Can Read! books published by Zonderkidz. From books your child reads with you to the first books he or she reads alone, there are I Can Read! books for every stage of reading:

SHARED READING
Basic language, word repetition, and whimsical illustrations, ideal for sharing with your emergent reader.

BEGINNING READING
Short sentences, familiar words, and simple concepts for children eager to read on their own.

READING WITH HELP
Engaging stories, longer sentences, and language play for developing readers.

READING ALONE
Complex plots, challenging vocabulary, and high-interest topics for the independent reader.

ADVANCED READING
Short paragraphs, chapters, and exciting themes for the perfect bridge to chapter books.

I Can Read! books have introduced children to the joy of reading since 1957. Featuring award-winning authors and illustrators and a fabulous cast of beloved characters, I Can Read! books set the standard for beginning readers.

A lifetime of discovery begins with the magical words **"I Can Read!"**

Visit www.icanread.com for information on enriching your child's reading experience.
Visit www.zonderkidz.com for more Zonderkidz I Can Read! titles.

Nothing at all can ever separate us
from God's love because of what
Christ Jesus our Lord has done.
—Romans 8:39

ZONDERKIDZ

Adam and Eve, God's First People

Copyright © 2010 by Zondervan
Illustrations © 2010 by Dennis G. Jones

Requests for information should be addressed to:

Zonderkidz, *Grand Rapids, Michigan* 49530

Library of Congress Cataloging-in-Publication Data
Jones, Dennis.
    Adam and Eve, God's first people / pictures by Dennis Jones.
       p.   cm.
    Summary: Retells, in illustrations and simple text, the biblical story of Genesis,
from the creation of light through the explusion from Eden.
    ISBN 978-0-310-71883-3 (softcover)
    [1. Creation—Fiction 2. God—Fiction. 3. Adam (Biblical figure)—Fiction.
4. Eve (Biblical figure)—Fiction.] I. Title.
PZ7.J6835Ad 2010
[E]—dc22   2009004132

Published in association with the literary agency of Alive Communica-
tions, Inc., 7680 Goddard Street #200, Colorado Springs, CO 80920.
www.alivecommunications.com

Zonderkidz is a trademark of Zondervan.

Editor: Mary Hassinger
Art direction: Sarah Molegraaf

Printed in China

10 11 12 13 14 15 /SCC/ 6 5 4 3

ADAM and EVE
God's First People

pictures by Dennis G. Jones

A long time ago,

everything was dark.

God was all by himself.

He decided to make things
to fill the darkness.

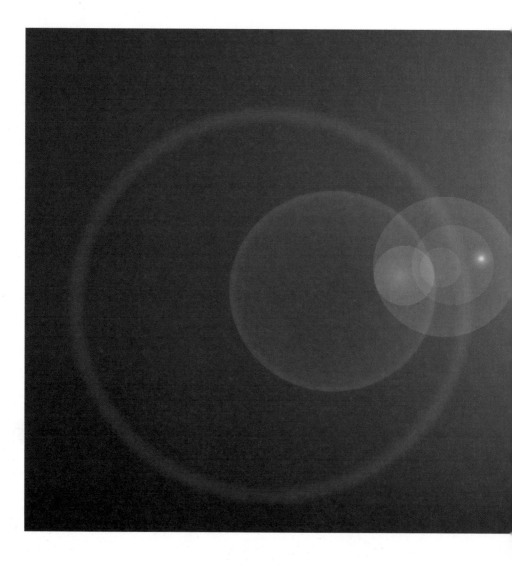

God didn't want it to be dark

all the time.

So he said, "Let there be light."

The light started to shine.

God called the light "day."

He called the dark "night."

This was the first day!

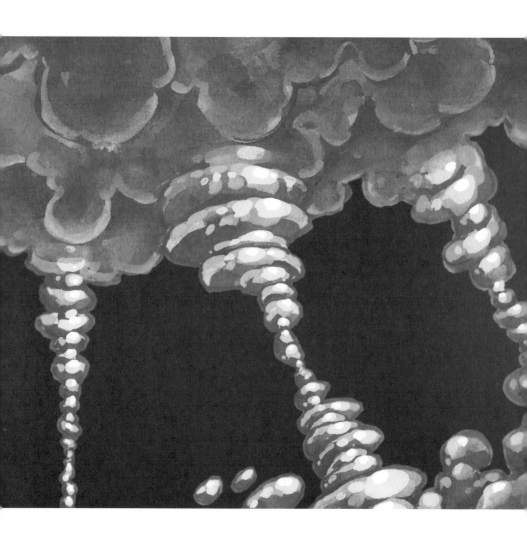

There was water everywhere.

It had always been there.

God wanted to keep the water apart.

On the second day,

God made a big space between the water.

He called the space "sky."

There was water above the sky

and water below the sky.

On the third day,

God looked at the water below the sky.

The water needed something in it.

God said, "Let dry ground appear."

And it did! God called it "land."

The land needed something too.

So God created plants and trees.

God liked the way everything looked.

It was very good.

On the fourth day,

God looked at the sky.

He made a big light called the sun

to shine during the day.

The sun made things warm and bright.

He made the moon and the stars

to shine during the night.

The moon and stars told the earth

when to sleep.

It was all very good.

On the fifth day,

God started to make animals.

He made birds to fly in the sky.

He made fish to swim in the water.

On the sixth day, God made more
animals to live on the land.

He made big lions and messy pigs.

God also made people on the sixth day.

God first made a man named Adam.

Later, God made a woman named Eve.

Adam and Eve took care of God's world.

And everything was very, very good.

God loved Adam and Eve.

He gave them a garden to live in
called Eden.

Eden was perfect.

18

Adam and Eve had all they needed.

And there was only one rule:

Don't eat from the tree of good and evil.

One day, Adam and Eve were walking
with the animals.

Eve heard a voice from one of the trees.

She stopped. It was the snake.

The snake wanted Adam and Eve

to break God's rule.

He decided to trick Eve.

The snake asked,

"Did God tell you not to eat fruit?"

Eve said, "God told us

we can eat fruit.

But we can't eat from the tree

of good and evil.

If we eat that fruit, we'll die."

The snake lied to Eve. He said,

"You can eat that fruit.

God is keeping a secret from you."

Eve looked at the tree.

The fruit looked very yummy.

Eve reached for the fruit

on the tree of good and evil.

It made the snake happy.

Eve took a BIG bite of the fruit.

The snake knew God would be sad.

The snake smiled.

Eve told Adam,

"The fruit on the tree of good and evil

tastes very good. Eat some."

So Adam ate the fruit too.

After Adam and Eve ate the fruit,

everything changed.

They saw they did not have clothes.

Eden was not perfect anymore.

Adam and Eve heard God coming.

They tried to hide from God.

God saw them and said,

"Adam and Eve, did you eat the fruit

I told you not to eat?"

Adam said, "Eve gave me the fruit."

Eve said, "The snake told me to eat it."

God was very sad.

His people had sinned.

Now bad things would happen to them.

God told Adam and Eve to leave Eden.

They couldn't live there because of sin.

But God had a plan.

His son, Jesus, would come to earth

and save us from sin.